The Flowers' Festival

Elsa Beskow

First published in Swedish as *Blomsterfesten* in 1914
First published in English in 1991 by Floris Books, 21 Napier Road. Edinburgh
© Bonniers Juniorförlag AB, 1986 English version © Joan Tate, 1991
British Library CIP data available   ISBN 0-86315-120-5   Printed in Italy

Floris Books

Lisa and her grandmother lived on the edge of the wood in a cottage with a garden all round it. Beyond the garden was their vegetable patch and a meadow sloping down to the lake, where the water lilies were just out. Behind the cottage was the real forest, full of twinflowers, bilberries and wintergreen.

Lisa had spent all Midsummer Eve working in the garden while Grandma tidied up the cottage. Then Grandma went out for a while, so Lisa sat down on the step and just gazed at all those sweet-smelling flowers. She could hear cheerful voices from people on their way to the Midsummer dance. She would have liked to go with them, but Grandma said she couldn't go alone.

"You'll just have to spend your Midsummer with the flowers," she said.

As she sat looking at the flowers, Lisa decided there was something special about them that evening. They almost seemed to be looking at her, trying to speak to her.

"What do you want?" she said, but they didn't answer.

Lisa ran out into the meadow to pick some wild flowers, and they were just the same — they kept nodding strangely at her. She lay down in the grass and nodded back — at the harebells, marguerites and buttercups. Then suddenly she heard someone call her by name, and, startled, she looked up.

"It's all right," said a gentle voice. "You needn't be afraid."

When Lisa looked up, she saw a beautiful figure standing in front of her. She had never seen anything like it before.

"I'm the Midsummer Fairy," the voice went on. "The flowers would like you to come to their party. You see, every Midsummer they can go where they like, though people can't see them, of course. If I put a drop of poppy-juice into your eyes, you'll be invisible, too, then you'll be able to see them. Would you like that?"

"Yes, please," said Lisa in surprise. "But why do I have to be invisible?"

"Some of them might be frightened if you weren't," said the fairy. "Because they're tiny compared with you. Close your eyes now."

Lisa closed her eyes and felt two drops fall on her eyelids. When she looked up again, the fairy had vanished.

But the meadow was full of life, because the flowers were all getting ready for the party. Lisa could see a family of buttercups eating their sandwiches, their mother very busy wiping the butter off their chins.

Lisa went back into the garden and found all the flowers bustling about. In the vegetable garden Mrs Potato and Mrs Beetroot were busy preparing the food — honey-dew and sweet-smelling pollen — and the Radishes, Carrots and Pea-blossom were all running around with plates piled high with food.

Then the first guests started arriving, the Cornflower leading the way with the Barley Boys to music from the crickets and bees. Behind her came marguerites, poppies and clover, hedge-roses, baby's slipper and timothy, camomile and wild chervil, bindweed and melanpyrum, harebells, buttercups and anthemies, speedwell and ragged robin, vetch, catchfly and wild pansies — so many, it was almost impossible to count them. The bees and the bumblebees buzzed, the crickets played and the harebells tinkled.

Then all the flowers of the forest came in a much quieter procession, led by the butterfly orchis. Behind came three twinflowers hand in hand, then the lovely spotted orchis, followed by the wild strawberry and her children. Then maianthemum, sorrel, bilberry and cranberry, and the club-moss with his long train. Behind him came the spruce and pine cones, and last of all a lively little juniper.

Every now and again, they stopped and called "Wintergreen, Wintergreen," back into the forest. But Wintergreen didn't come at first, so they went on into the garden.

At the top of the garden, Queen Rose was sitting on her throne welcoming all the guests, surrounded by her court — Lady Pansy, Lady Peony, Lady Lilac and Lady Honeysuckle, Lord Crown Imperial and Lord Bleeding Heart, Sir Iris, a pretty little Columbine and two little Daisy chambermaids.

"How wonderful that you all managed to be ready on time," said the Rose, smiling at them. They smiled back and bowed and curtsied.

"Play up!" cried the Queen Rose to her musicians, clapping her hands. The cricket, the bees and bumblebees at once struck up a cheerful tune and the Dew-cups and Pea-blossom ran around with refreshments.

Last of all came the flowers from the lake and the marshy meadow around it, the Common Reed, the lovely Flowering Rush, Pondweed, Cotton grass and Miss Calla, then one small Cloudberry flower with a single cloudberry as a gift. Behind them came the Geums and Forget-Me-Nots and a Yellow Water Lily in bud, then Mr Rush and the handsome, young Yellow Flag.

"Where's my cousin Queen Water Lily?" said the rose, "I did so want to meet her."

"Your Majesty," said the Reed, bowing low. "She sends her thanks and best wishes, but says she is afraid she can't come, because she can only breathe in the lake."

Then the door of the cottage opened and to Lisa's surprise, all the house plants started cautiously coming down the steps, the two Miss Pelargoniums first, then plump little Mrs Myrtle, followed by grand Lady Fuchsia.

"Welcome to the party!" cried the flowers.

"Thank you kindly," said Lady Fuchsia. "We very much wanted to come, but we were afraid of draughts and the cold night air."

Queen Rose gave Lady Fuchsia her best cobweb shawl and asked her to sit beside her.

"Now please, all of you," called the Queen. "Find a seat and the story-telling can start. I hope everyone's here."

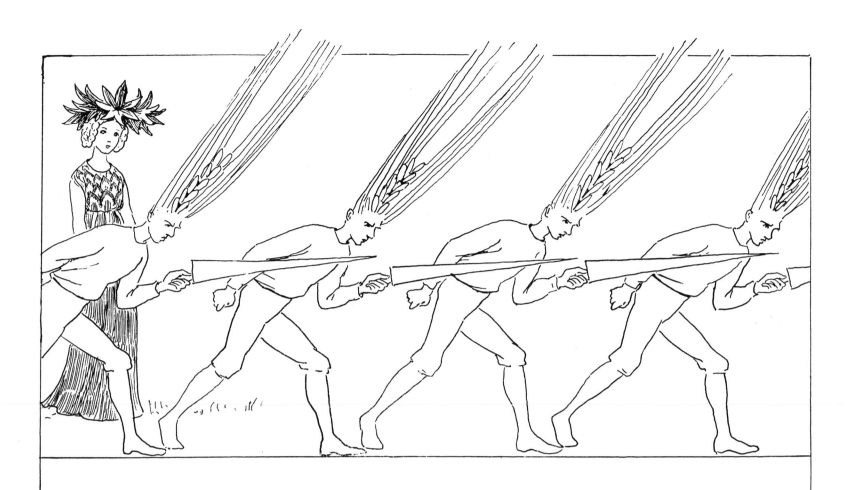

As she spoke, there was a terrible hubbub at the gate, because a whole crowd of weeds was trying to get in. But the Carrots and Beetroots were furious and wouldn't let them.

"What's all the noise about?" cried the Rose.

"Weeds!" said Mrs Beetroot. "Scoundrels and beggars and ragamuffins, all trying to get in. We'll soon put a stop to that! We'd never get rid of them if we let them in."

"Hear, hear," cried all the other vegetables.

"But we're flowers, too," cried the weeds. "We're no worse than that Cornflower."

"What?" cried the Barley Boys. "How can you be compared with the proud Cornflower? Rabble! Be off with you!"

"Now, now," said the Rose. "Calm down a little. Please, no quarrelling on Midsummer Eve."

"I suggest," she said to the weeds, "that you sit along the edge of the ditch outside the garden. Then you can hear and see just as well, as long as you sit quite still and don't disturb the party. The Dew-cups will bring you refreshments and perhaps Mr Thistle would be so kind as to stand guard at the gate?"

"Certainly, your Majesty," said the Thistle. "I'll deal with any troublemakers."

At that, calm was restored, and the story-telling could begin.

A bumblebee buzzed up to the Rose, followed by a shy Bird's-Foot Trefoil.

"Your Majesty," said the bumblebee, "I have a little story I hope you will like. It's about this little flower-child here."

And this is the bumblebee's story:

One day, I was buzzing and humming and zooming from flower to flower in the meadow, and I came across a little yellow flower, the Bird's-Foot Trefoil, crying her eyes out.

"What's the matter, little flower?" I said. "Why are you crying on such a fine day as this?"

But the little Trefoil just went on crying.

"The sun is out," I said, "and everyone's happy. Tell me what's wrong?"

"I know, I know," she said tearfully. "I can hear them all singing. I can walk about like them in my pretty yellow skirt but ..."

"But what?" I said.

"You see," she said. "I am just as pretty as they are, but they call me a vetch. It sounds like a witch. And scorpion vetch at that, so nobody likes me at all."

"Oh, is that all," I said. "We can soon put that right. We'll call you Senna instead. Do you like that?"

"Oh, yes," said the little flower.

And she dried her tears and joined in with the others.

"Very pretty," said Queen Rose. "She can keep that name."

And the meadow flowers lifted the Bird's-Foot Trefoil, the lovely Princess Senna up into the air and cried "Long Live Princess Senna!"

"Perhaps it's my turn now," said the garden warbler, peeping out of a lilac bush. "I saw something really nice at the party, so I at once made up a story about it."

On the day of the party, all the little Violets were dressed in their very best for the party, when along came their rich relation, Madame Pansy. Oh, how grand she was in her long rich velvet gown and beautiful yellow collar, a tiara on her handsome head. She held her head high and spoke firmly to her small relations.

"Calm down, little ones," she said. "And line up nicely, so I can pay my respects to the Queen."

The Violets obediently got into line and Madame Pansy started practising her walk and her curtsey.

But, oh dear, that beautiful rich velvet gown was rather long and suddenly — plop! — and Madame Pansy tripped over it and fell flat on her face.

The violets tried hard not to laugh and rushed over to help Madame Pansy to her feet again.

"Thank you, thank you," said Madame Pansy, not quite so haughtily. "But whatever shall I do if that happens again?"

The Violets put their heads together, then one of them said: "I know, we'll get the Viola Twins to hold up your train, and then you'll be safe."

That's just what they did.

And ever since then, Madame Pansy has been much nicer to her small half-brothers and sisters.

Then along came the goldfinch with his story. "I made it up in the park," he said.

And this is his story:

Mrs Chestnut in her snowy white gown lives in the tops of the spreading horse chestnut tree with her sisters. At Midsummer, they are in full bloom and reign all over the tree, their gowns like pyramid candles pointing to the sky.

Mrs Chestnut has a great many sons, all of them brave young knights and warriors, with lances and spiky green armour. But at the moment, it is Mrs Chestnut's turn to dream in the warmth of the sun and the bright blue sky.

For she knows that when all her blooms have gone and she has withered away, when autumn comes and the wind blows wildly, loosening her green leaves and whirling them up in the air, all her sons will ride away in their shining armour, their lances at the ready.

Then when the battle with the wind is over and all the brave warriors have fallen, their armour splits wide open and there they are — brown and glossy, hard and firm, all ready to be collected and brought home for this year's games of conkers.

"Oh, that was beautiful," sighed Queen Rose, wiping away a tear.

Then a chaffinch came hopping along.

"Perhaps my story sounds rather simple after that," he said. "But it's about what ordinary people feel."

And this is the chaffinch's story:

Mrs Broad Bean had three babies and she made them a long green cradle and tucked them up inside the cradle in a soft green blanket. Then she rocked them and rocked them and sang them all to sleep.

"Rockabye, rockabye, sleep warm and tight," she sang. "Then one day when you've grown big and strong, I'll let you all go."

She kept them warm and cosy, rocking them to sleep every night and waking them up in the morning when the sun rose. They grew and grew and soon filled the whole of their cradle.

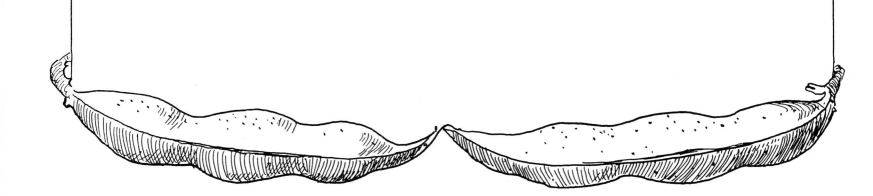

One day she said to them: "Now it's time for you to go out into the big wide world. There they will plant you deep down in the warm earth, then next year you, too, will grow, and grow, and grow.

"Then you, too, will each have an armful of green babies, and you, too, will make a cradle and rock them, and rock them, until they are big and strong and can ...

"... go out into the big wide world."

"Marvellous," cried all the vegetables. "That story should have the first prize!"

"We haven't heard them all yet," said Queen Rose. "We've heard nothing from the forest."

"I have a story from the forest," said the thrush. "But I'm afraid it's not as jolly as the others."

And this is the thrush's story:

Wintergreen has another name: Pyrola, and she is a shy, timid little forest flower, who hides away and even at Midsummer, it is difficult to persuade her to join in the festivities. That is why you hear the forest flowers calling her when it is time to go to the party.

"Pyrola, Pyrola," they call. "Beautiful Wintergreen, come now."

But the Wintergreen hides her lovely head in dark corners of the forest, and keeps herself away from the sun.

This Midsummer, five little twinflowers sang a song for her:

Wintergreen, Wintergreen, look up at the sun.
Wintergreen, Wintergreen, come join in the fun.
Princess Pyrola, come to the dance,
Summer is short and here is your chance.
Wintergreen, Wintergreen, come to the dance.

And she did.

"You know what," the shrill voice of a cheeky sparrow suddenly piped up. "Let's have something more cheerful. I suggest something I've just thought up. I think maybe my friends outside the gate will like it."

This is his story:

Once upon a time, there was a great gang of raggedy, higgledy piggledy weeds, all poor, all noisy, all cheerful and not at all good. They were all different, big weeds, little weeds, middle-sized weeds, Chickweed, Thistles, Groundsel, Dandelions, Burdock and multitudes of others. An army of them, always at the ready, always full of fun.

One day, they held a meeting. King Dandelion was chairman and Old Mrs Nettle kept order.

"We're sick of being pulled up as soon as we've grown," shouted the Dandelions.

"We're sick of being slashed and burnt," yelled the Nettles. "They hardly even let us flower."

"We're sick of being dug up as soon as we peep out of the earth," they all shouted at once. "And then they throw us on the compost heap like so much rubbish."

"But you know?" said King Dandelion. "We're stronger than they are. We don't mind the hot sun, or the cold winds. Whatever they do, we always manage to come up again."

"I know," said the Chickweed. "Let's have a party of our own."

So they did. A very noisy party, a very friendly party, with lots of wild dancing and banging of drums and blowing of trumpets.

The garden flowers heard them and said to themselves: "Here they come again, that idle crowd of ragamuffins. Will we never be rid of them?"

The answer came back in a great ragamuffin roar: "NO!"

When the sparrow's song was over, there was another roar, this time of applause from the weeds outside the gate.

But the vegetables all hissed loudly.

"What a story for our party," said Lady Peony indignantly to Queen Rose. "Can't you get rid of all that rabble?"

A Burdock boy clinging to the fence hurled prickly burrs at the flowers and they got caught in their dresses. The ladies made a fearful fuss and Lady Fuchsia fainted away, Mrs Myrtle screamed for the police, and the two knights Sir Iris and Lord Bleeding Heart drew their swords.

Queen Rose tried to calm them down, but couldn't even make herself heard. Then the thistle took the Burdock by the scruff of his neck and lifted him up.

"Here's the culprit," he cried in his deep voice. "Shall I spike him through?"

"No, no," said Queen Rose. "That'd be far too harsh."

"Perhaps we'd better chase him away," said some of the weeds.

Old Mrs Nettle pushed her way through the gate and creakingly curtsied to the Queen.

"With permission, your Majesty," she said, "I'll see the boy gets a good thrashing. I've done that before."

Mrs Nettle grabbed the poor Burdock and dragged him off.

"Now let's have something to calm us all down," said the Rose, cooling herself with her fan.

"Perhaps I can be of service," said a frog, hopping up. "I can sing you a song, a song that will calm everyone down. It's a lullaby and also a cooling song, because it's all about water."

When the frog began to sing, Lisa noticed the flowers all nodding off one by one, then falling asleep. Before she could think what was happening, she too had fallen asleep, and she slept so soundly she didn't wake up until Grandma lifted her up and carried her into the cottage.

So the Midsummer party was over. But long after the flowers had all fallen asleep, the frog could still be heard singing his song:

Lullaby waves, slowly washing ashore,
Sing lullaby, sweet lullaby,
Gently rippling, rolling ashore,
Sing lullaby, sweet lullaby.

The day is over,
The long day is done,
Heads on to pillows,
Sleep now to come.

The reeds in the bay
In the evening wind,
Rustle and sway,
Whispering their tune

Tail, fin, and gill
In the depths of the lake,
The silver fish still,
Not a sound they make.

The water lily children
Closed for the night,
Bobbing their heads,
Awaiting the light.

Still is the water,
Still is the shore,
Still is the mist
On the meadow floor.

Only the nightjar
Calls in the night:
"The midnight hour is here.
The midnight hour is here."